KT-447-735

THIS BOOK
BELONGS TO

....

WHO IS A VERY

RESPONSIBLE

CHILD.

*I celebrated World Book Day 2019 with
this gift from my local bookseller and
HarperCollins Children's Books.*

#ShareAStory

LAUREN CHILD

IS CREATOR OF THE PHENOMENALLY
SUCCESSFUL AND BAFTA-WINNING
Charlie and Lola series, as well as the
globally bestselling Clarice Bean series.
She has sold millions of books around the
world and won several prizes – including
the Smarties Prize (four times) and the
highly respected Kate Greenaway Medal.
Hubert Horatio began life as a picture-
book character. Lauren is the current
Waterstones Children's Laureate.

CELEBRATE STORIES. LOVE READING.

This book has been specially written and published to celebrate World Book Day. We are a charity who offers every child and young person the opportunity to read and love books by giving you the chance to have a book of your own. To find out more, and for oodles of fun activities and reading recommendations to continue your reading journey, visit **worldbookday.com**

World Book Day in the UK and Ireland is made possible by generous sponsorship from National Book Tokens, participating publishers, booksellers, authors and illustrators. The £1* book tokens are a gift from your local bookseller.

World Book Day works in partnership with a number of charities, all of whom are working to encourage a love of reading for pleasure.

* €1.50 in Ireland

The National Literacy Trust is an independent charity that encourages children and young people to enjoy reading. Just ten minutes of reading every day can make a big difference to how well you do at school and to how successful you could be in life. **literacytrust.org.uk**

The Reading Agency inspires people of all ages and backgrounds to read for pleasure and empowerment. They run the Summer Reading Challenge in partnership with libraries; they also support reading groups in schools and libraries all year round. Find out more and join your local library. **summerreadingchallenge.org.uk**

World Book Day also facilitates fundraising for:

Book Aid International, an international book donation and library development charity. Every year, they provide one million books to libraries and schools in communities where children would otherwise have little or no opportunity to read. **bookaid.org**

Read for Good, which motivates children in schools to read for fun through its sponsored read, which thousands of schools run on World Book Day and throughout the year. The money raised provides new books and resident storytellers in all the children's hospitals in the UK. **readforgood.org**

First published
in Great Britain
by
HarperCollins *Children's Books* in 2019
HarperCollins *Children's Books* is a division of HarperCollins*Publishers* Ltd,
HarperCollins Publishers
1 London Bridge Street
London SE1 9GF
The HarperCollins website address is
www.harpercollins.co.uk

1

ISBN 978–0–00–832743–9

Lauren Child asserts the moral right to be identified
as the author and illustrator of the work.
A CIP catalogue record for this title is available from the British Library.

Based on original text design by David Mackintosh
Printed and bound in England by CPI Group (UK) Ltd, Croydon, CR0 4YY

LAUREN CHILD

HUBERT HORATIO

A Very Fishy Tale

HarperCollins Children's Books

sider this a
ish Classic

Lauren is
Laureate!

World Book Day works in
partnership with a number of
charities, all of whom are
working to encourage a love of
reading for pleasure.

CHILD:
N BOOKS

MON
IN HIS

UL AND BAFTA-WINNING
g Clarice Bean series.

CHIPS

WINNER OF VACUUM
CLEANS UP IN VOUCH
COMPETITIO

WORLD CUP
HAND OF COD: WINNER TAKES A

ACQUES
ECTION

roved
y secto

and chips

oggy
of fish

The Bobton-Trent family has fallen on hard
financial times. They have had to sell off all
their most valuable
leave their

es for a
report.

NDERS
NG FOR

MO
IN

IMPROVES
SAYS

PREFACE

THIS STORY IS SET IN THE PAST — in those *carefree* years long before the Bobton-Trent family had fallen on hard financial times. Before they'd had to sell off all their most valuable possessions and so leave their mansion, Sweeping Acres, for pastures new — otherwise known as number 17b Plankton Heights.

This story is from the days when the Bobton-Trents had it cushy, very cushy indeed.

Yes, those days were the days.

I

Meet...

the Bobton-Trents

MR AND MRS BOBTON-TRENT LOVED PEOPLE.

THEY LOVED EATING IN RESTAURANTS AND conversing with the diners who happened to be sitting at adjacent tables. They loved bumping into friends in the park. They loved bumping into strangers in the street. They were happy when talking with the woman who came to clean the pool filter and they were happy when laughing

with the man who came to shampoo the carpets.

They adored meeting anyone and everyone, but

the person they adored

the most was their

one and only

child . . .

HUBERT HORATIO

BARTLE

BOBTON-

TRENT.

He was remarkable. An interesting child: peculiarly mature for his age, keen to have a go at *everything*, very *clever* and delighted to talk to *anyone*. AND he was responsible. Very, *very* responsible.

PERHAPS YOU'RE ASKING YOURSELF JUST HOW HUBERT CAME TO BE SUCH AN EXCEPTIONALLY RESPONSIBLE CHILD?

The answer is it really has a great deal to do with his parents being EXCEPTIONALLY IRRESPONSIBLE *grown-ups.*

PICTURE OF HUBERT AGED 1¾, HAVING SAVED HIS OWN LIFE FOR THE FIFTH TIME!

II

A
Very
Fishy
Tale

i.

Hubert's First Outing in a Pram

IT WAS A LOVELY APRIL DAY AND THE BIRDS WERE
all singing and there was plenty to look at —
and Mr and Mrs Bobton-Trent *loved* looking.
Particularly, they loved looking in windows, any
windows, though they had a special fascination
for shop windows. Shop windows, you see, are
the best sort of windows to look in if you happen
to be the kind of people who like to buy things.

And the Bobton-Trents were

very ENTHUSIASTIC
buyers of
THINGS.

However, on this particular spring day, Mr
and Mrs Bobton-Trent had been very restrained.
They had stopped to look at many window

displays, they had admired all the various things and had commented on how desirable everything looked and had mentioned just how much they might like to own whatever it was they were looking *at* . . . BUT they had NOT stepped inside a single store because on *this particular day* Hubert's parents wanted to show their baby son all the wonderful things it is possible to delight in without spending a single cent, penny, rouble, krone or yen – i.e. a lot can be enjoyed for free and it is important to remember that.

For example:

looking at NATURE,
at T R E E S and

flowers,

at *people* and *animals* and insects, at

CLOUD SHAPES and grass, at cars

and buildings and holes in the road. And what

the Bobton-Trents knew was that if you take

the trouble to look then it is not unusual to *find*

things. And the Bobton-Trents were *always*

finding things, all sorts of things – sometimes

discarded on purpose, sometimes accidentally lost

from pockets or forgotten on benches.

Most of the things they found they took home
(at least the found things that were neither
smelly nor revolting nor obviously rubbish),
and this made for an INTERESTING
collection.

#268:
Die, see-through
Interest: high

#0I0:
Specs, polarising
Interest: extremely high

#063:
Monkey, squeaky
Interest: low

#000:
(Unclassified)
Interest: ?

#051:

Star, cubic zirconia

Interest: high

#008:

Earring, drop

Interest: medium

#222:

Badge, novelty

Interest: low

#320:

Shoe, corrective

Interest: medium

#679:

Leopard's mouth

Interest: v. high

#014:

Leopard, polymer

Interest: v. v. high

ii.

The Silver Voucher

ANYWAY, BACK TO THAT APRIL DAY...

IT WAS AT HALF PAST THREE IN THE AFTERNOON when Mr Bobton-Trent caught sight of something silver and papery snagged in an ornamental rosebush outside the hairdresser's at the bottom of Hill Crest Slope.

"Ooh," said Mrs Bobton-Trent as her husband reached to retrieve the silver thing.

"What is it?" she asked.

"I think it's something good," he said,

examining the

message on

the SILVER card.

WHOSOEVER FINDS THIS
SILVER VOUCHER MAY SELECT

One Item*

absolutely free from the household-wares department situated on the lower ground floor of the renowned department store,

Billings & Grimpton's

222 HILL CREST SLOPE

* to the value of £3.99

34

"How wonderful," said Mrs Bobton-Trent.

Mr Bobton-Trent handed the silver card to his baby son and said, "Look, Hubert, it really is our lucky day!"

They turned the pram in the direction of Billings & Grimpton's and began climbing the steep hill, and baby Hubert, fearing the voucher would get caught by the wind, tucked it sensibly into his baby sailor suit.

When they reached the shop Mrs Bobton-Trent wondered what they should choose.

"We don't really need any more household appliances," she said. "What would be the point in acquiring another vacuum cleaner?

As seen through the Billings & Grimpton's picture window.

we already have twenty-three of them, and I've lost count of the number of waffle-makers we own." She paused as a very good idea popped into her head.

"Let's give the voucher away!" she suggested. "Someone might be very pleased to have £79.99 to spend on a household appliance."

"Brilliant idea!" agreed her husband.

But where *was* the silver voucher?

"Oh dear," said Mr Bobton-Trent,

looking down at Hubert, "I think our darling son must have eaten it."

Baby Hubert said nothing because he was distracted by a cloud that looked exactly like an Irish wolfhound.

Mrs Bobton-Trent looked at her watch. "He must be hungry — after all, it *is* nearly four o'clock in the afternoon."

"High time for tea," agreed Mr Bobton-Trent. "We should get home before Grimshaw sounds the xylophone."

But, just as they were turning to leave, his eye was caught by something golden and shiny.

"Oh, my! Do you see what I see?"

And then Mrs Bobton-Trent saw it too.

"Oh, I do."

There, in one of the many beautiful Billings & Grimpton's window displays, was something so necessary, something so useful, something so, so, *so* shiny and golden that both Bobton-Trents clasped their hands together with delight, so

letting

go

of

Hubert's

pram.

The label on the shiny gold thing said:

Billings & Grumptonis

A must-have for the child who has EVERYTHING

EXTREMELY USEFUL IN CASE OF EMERGENCY

"That's Hubert," said Mrs Bobton-Trent.

"Yes, he is certainly a child who has everything," agreed Mr Bobton-Trent, peering at the little object in the window.

In smallish print next to the shiny golden thing it said again:

EXTREMELY USEFUL
IN CASE OF EMERGENCY

"It could be a life-saver," said Mrs Bobton-Trent.

"That seals it," said Mr Bobton-Trent. "Hubert needs something in case of emergency."

"I agree," agreed Mrs Bobton-Trent. "I mean, what if he ever found himself lost?"

☛ iii.

Hubert Takes Charge

AND SO OFF THEY WENT...

LEAVING HUBERT HORATIO LYING IN HIS PRAM,

watching the clouds

m o v i n g

s l o w l y by . . .

Or not slowly, more sort of *quickly* —

very *fast* in fact. He gripped the sides of his

pram, pulled

himself up

and looked out.

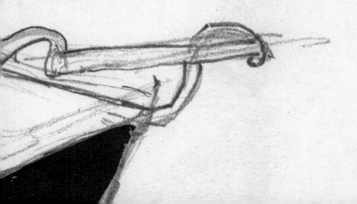

No, it was not the clouds that were moving

fast, it was *he* who was moving . . .

moving VERY FAST *indeed.*

Hubert peered out and was surprised to

find . . . himself *hurtling down*

Hill Crest Slope

towards Busy-Fourth Street.

Hill Crest Slope was actually
A VERY STEEP HILL
and Busy-Fourth Street was busy,

as its name suggested.

Baby Hubert immediately took charge

of the situation, steering the pram by

leaning his weight one way

and then the other.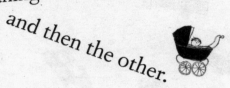

He **careered** through the traffic at great

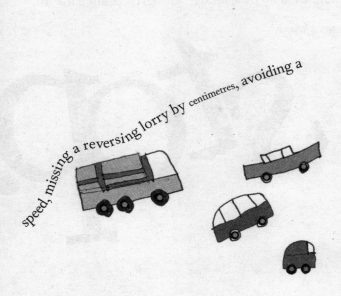

speed, missing a reversing lorry by centimetres, avoiding a

crocodile of school children

by millimetres . . .

and then all of a sudden Hubert's pram came to

an *abrupt*

stop.

up into the sky,

high

pram, before

the

out of plummeting down

catapulted

was

he not

that to

abrupt earth

So but

something

much wetter. SPLASH!

He was PLUnGEd into some VERY

cold and

freshwater

water.

☞ iv.

The Haddock

WHERE
AM I?

HE
WONDERED.

It didn't feel one bit like his bath. There were no soapy bubbles and no big hands to lift him out.

And what were those beady-eyed things with the large snappies?

They were waving. They looked *friendly*.

"How do you do?"

bubbled Hubert.

They *weren't* friendly.

They were very grabby. One of them pinched Hubert's nose much too tightly.

"Ow!" gasped Hubert.

The beady-eyed thing wouldn't let go. This wasn't Hubert's only problem. He suddenly realised that he couldn't seem to breathe.

It must be something to do with the water, he decided. He had heard the grown-ups talking about being careful not to go under the water because of the drowning, and he realised that maybe the drowning was what was happening now, in which case it didn't seem like a good idea. Breathing, he realised, must be more important than he had first thought.

He managed to detach himself from the grabber by using a tickling technique he had learned from his parents (everyone has a tickle point). Next he noticed a large floating rope ladder, which stretched down into the water and upwards out into the air, and Hubert, who was an excellent crawler, began to crawl. He was making good progress on his own, but then some kind person pulled

the ladder upwards

and he was heaved

out of the wet and on to

a wooden floor.

Lots of slimy, slappy, flippy things had also been heaved out and were opening and closing their mouths, but no words were coming out.

Hubert, together with the flippy things, was scooped into a giant bucket and carried off.

It was rather smelly in the bucket and he was relieved when he was at long last tipped out on to a large metal tray on top of an outdoor table.

Had he not been buried under so many of the flippy things, he would have been able to see the flappy green-and-white material above him. And had Hubert ever gone shopping with Zelda the cook, he would have known he was now at the food market, on the fish stall, underneath several haddock.

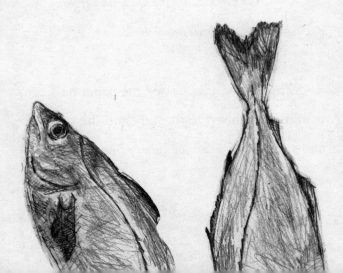

"A LARGE haddock, please," said a lady.

A gloved hand felt around, squeezed Hubert's chubby tummy, yanked him out of the fish pile and quickly wrapped him in paper. The fishmonger didn't notice that this fish was NOT a fish because he was too busy being distracted by a cloud that looked almost exactly like a dumbo octopus.*

[* THIS IS A REAL SPECIES OF OCTOPUS, *by the way, and if you don't believe me look it up.*]

The fishmonger passed the paper package containing Hubert to the lady and she smiled and said, "This is a nice heavy one," and she

carefully popped him in her wheelie basket and
began walking towards the bus stop. She hadn't
got far when she heard a voice.

"Excuse me!"

THE LADY STOPPED and looked around.

Where was the voice coming from? It sounded muffled, almost like the mutterings of someone tightly wrapped in paper.

"Excuse me! Do you mind?"

There it was again. It seemed to be coming from her shopping basket.

"I need to get to Billings and Grimpton's department store," said the voice. The lady didn't know what to say — it was embarrassing to talk to one's wheelie basket.

"Hello?" called the voice.

"Hello?" replied the lady uncertainly. It was either the cauliflower or one of the potatoes . . . or maybe . . . the haddock.

"I would take a taxi, but I haven't got my wallet with me," said the voice.

The lady decided it must be the haddock. It seemed very unlikely that a cauliflower would own a wallet.

"My parents will worry about me if I'm not

there when they come back for me," said the haddock.

The lady felt it was wise to do whatever a talking fish asked you to do. *It might have magical powers*, she thought. *If this were a fairy tale, then a talking haddock would definitely have magical powers*. She thought perhaps it might grant her three wishes; she could do with a new vacuum cleaner.

So she crossed the road and began climbing Hill Crest Slope, dragging her trolley behind her. She was getting a little out of breath. She hoped the effort was going to be worth it; her ingrowing toenail was playing up again.

When they reached the shop, the lady said, "*Now* what should I do?"

"Thank you!"

"Would you mind putting me down
just outside the revolving doors?" said the fish.
"I'm sure they'll look for me here."

The lady set him down on the pavement.

"So, can I have my three wishes?" she asked.

Hubert wasn't certain that he could do
wishes. *Do babies do wishes?* he wondered – oh
dear, maybe they did.

"I don't know," said the fish.

71

"It's customary to get THREE wishes," said the lady rather firmly. "I read about it in a book."

She sounded like she knew what she was talking about so Hubert said, "Well, in that case I'll try my best, but don't get cross if I can't manage more than one. I've never done this before."

The lady nodded and closed her eyes.

"I wish I could have a new vacuum cleaner," she said.

"I can do that," said the fish, "but I will need my arms."

"That's a nuisance," said the lady, because of course fish don't have arms and now she feared that she would not get even *one* of her wishes.

72

It was turning out to be a very difficult day and, what's more, an embarrassing one.

"I wish you had arms," said the lady, looking around her. She thought she saw Mrs Stansbury on the other side of the road.

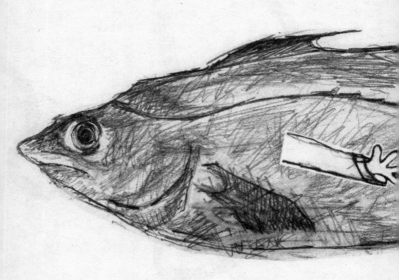

Mrs Stansbury was a dreadful gossip.

"Oh dear," she said, closing her eyes, "it will be all round the neighbourhood – I wish you weren't a fish."

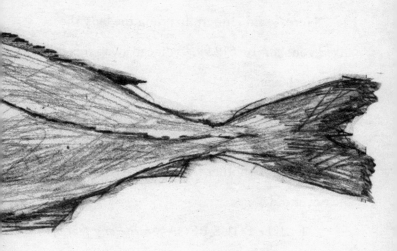

☞ *You may have wondered where fish fingers come from . . .*

While she was still fretting, Hubert was tearing his way out of the parcel and by the time the lady opened her eyes there was a fish with arms sitting in a pile of fishy paper. *No*, not a *fish* with arms but a baby in a sailor suit, and what was that he was holding in his little hands?

"Here," said Hubert, handing the lady the silver voucher for £79.99, "you can swap this for a vacuum cleaner."

The lady was amazed.

"Thank you," she said. "I wish to goodness that I never eat another fish again." (And, actually, she never did.)

[AND THUS BEGAN *a lifelong fear of haddock for both parties.*]

A minute or so later Mr and Mrs Bobton-Trent appeared.

"What have you done with the pram, darling Hubert Horatio?"

It was hard to know where the pram could be now. And Hubert rather suspected that it might not be in such good working order and therefore thought it best to say nothing. Explaining things can mean having to answer an awful lot of tricky questions.

"Pram thieves," said his father.

"Such a shame," said his mother. "But at least you are safe. Prams are a dime a dozen and ten a penny, but you, dearest H, are

ONE
in a *million*."

"One *in a* TRILLION,"
corrected his father.

"Quite so," agreed his mother.

"PRICELESS!"

"If only you'd had this," said his father, handing him a little gold shiny thing, "this never would have happened."

"That's why we rushed in to buy it," said his mother.

"And not a moment too soon," said his father.

"A moment too late, in fact," said his mother.

"If only you'd had this dear little SOS whistle, you could have alerted us to your plight."

"Have you noticed he has a faint

odour

of

fish

about

him?"

said   his

father.

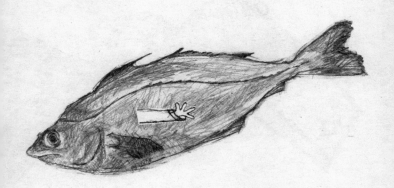

"It must be the *SHOCK*,"
said his mother.

She hung the whistle round Hubert's neck
and Hubert thought it was a very nice gold shiny
thing, even if the getting of it had just about
almost killed him.

☛ *Be Prepared for ANY Unexpected SOS Event with this Portable Acoustic Device. This lightweight, gold-plated reinforced silver one-pea emergency whistle with adjustable gingham neck sling can be deployed in an instant and operates using only one lungful of air. Caution: whistle emits the tone of high C in the upper decibels.*

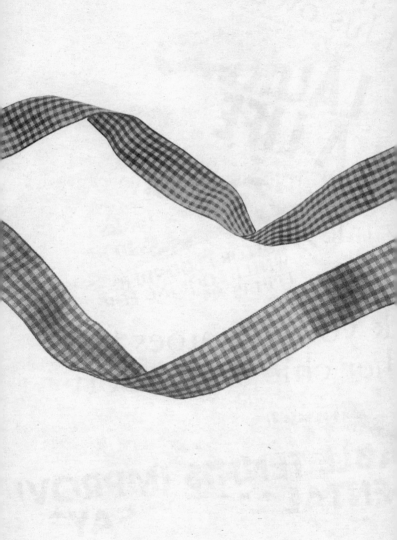

In a Cla

f his own

"Wry, inventive, whimsical" said
H... ...IO: HOW TO
I... ...UPS

LAUREI
A LIFE

CREATOR OF THE PHENOMENAL...
Charlie and Lola series, as well as the

l genu

y tale "

resting child: peculiarly
have a go at everything,
talk to anyone. And he
responsible.

looks i
s in pr

EDITOR FLOUNDERS
WHILE LOOKING FOR
FISH PUNS

k your potatoes for
her chip says report

more on page 37

ABLE TENNIS IMPROV
ENTAL M... ...
SAY

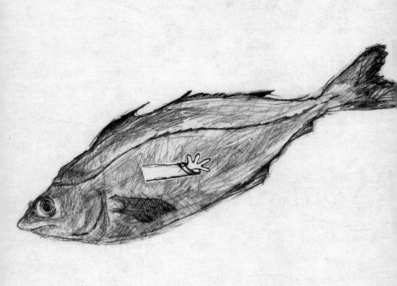

'WITTY, INVENTIVE AND WHIMSICAL' *Sunday Times*

LAUREN CHILD

HUBERT HORATIO
HOW to Raise your Grown-ups

A book *in* *a* MILLION

"WRY, INVENTIVE, whimsical"

Sunday Times

"Crammed with the Children's Laureate's DISTINCTIVE multilayered visual *humour*"

Guardian

SHARE A STORY

From breakfast to bedtime, there's always time to discover and share stories together. You can . . .

1 TAKE A TRIP to your LOCAL BOOKSHOP

Brimming with brilliant books and helpful booksellers to share awesome reading recommendations, you can also enjoy booky events with your favourite authors and illustrators.

 FIND YOUR LOCAL BOOKSHOP: booksellers.org.uk/ bookshopsearch

2 JOIN your LOCAL LIBRARY

That wonderful place where the hugest selection of books you could ever want to read awaits – and you can borrow them for FREE! Plus expert advice and fantastic free family reading events.

 FIND YOUR LOCAL LIBRARY: findmylibrary.co.uk

3 CHECK OUT the WORLD BOOK DAY WEBSITE

Looking for reading tips, advice and inspiration? There is so much for you to discover at **worldbookday.com**, packed with fun activities, games, downloads, podcasts, videos, competitions and all the latest new books galore.

SPONSORED BY

NATIONAL BOOK tokens

Illustrations © Rob Biddulph

Celebrate stories. Love reading.

WORLD
BOOK DAY

SHARE A STORY

Well **hello** there! We are

Overjoyed that you have **joined our celebration** of

Reading books and **sharing stories**, because we

Love bringing **books** to you.

Did you know, we are a **charity** dedicated to celebrating the

Brilliance of **reading for pleasure** for everyone, everywhere?

Our mission is to help you discover **brand new stories** and

Open your mind to exciting **new worlds** and **characters**, from

Kings and **queens** to **wizards** and **pirates** to **animals** and **adventurers** and so many more. We couldn't

Do it without all the amazing **authors** and **illustrators**, **booksellers** and **bookshops**, publishers, schools and **libraries** out there –

And most importantly, we couldn't do it all without . . .

YOU!

On your bookmarks, get set, READ!
Happy Reading. Happy World Book Day.